Geraldine McCaughrean

DOG DAYS

**Hodder
Children's
Books**

a division of Hodder Headline Limited

For Natalie

First published Great Britain in 2002
by Hodder Children's Books
This paperback edition published in 2004

A Catalogue record for this book is
available from the British Library

ISBN 0 340 86608 X

Typeset in Candida by Avon DataSet Ltd,
Bidford-on-Avon, Warwickshire

Printed and bound in Great Britain by
Clays Ltd, St Ives plc

The paper and board used in this paperback by Hodder Children's
Books are natural recyclable products made from wood grown in
sustainable forests. The manufacturing processes conform to the
environmental regulations of the country of origin.

Hodder Children's Books
A division of Hodder Headline Limited
338 Euston Rd, London NW1 3BH

for more information about the author please visit:
www.geraldinemccaughrean.co.uk

Contents

1

Thin Ice

She was the colour and size of a haystack with a brain the size of a needle. Why else would she have ventured out on to the ice when the river was thawing? Now she just stood, looking up at the houses on the bridge, and barking in a slow, tuneless rhythm, like an old man coughing. The ice was slippery. Her paws kept splaying outwards until the cold of the ice on her belly made her tiptoe back up to her full height. And still she barked. Someone on the bridge threw a lump of coal at her. It skidded across the whiteness, leaving a black trail, then plopped into a fissure: the ice was breaking up.

After yet another winter of breathtaking cold, the Thames was finally remembering its true nature. Growling like something much bigger than a dog, its ice buckled and broke. Soon the big animal was standing marooned on a diamond of slippery, rocking ice.

"We have to help her," said Clay. "The poor beast will drown!"

"It got out there. It can get back," said Hal doubtfully, but already he was tapping his foot on the ice, testing whether it would take his weight. The dog in the middle of the river was far too beautiful to abandon.

The muddy foreshore crackled under their feet like eggshell, then they were out on the frozen river, calling, all the time calling to the big dog. She turned and looked at the two brothers with sad, despairing eyes, as if to say, *"I would like to come, but my place is here . . ."* Then she went back to barking.

Slipping and teetering, jumping and skidding, Clay and Hal crossed cracks and gaps in the ice, which at once widened into canyons. Here and there, they glimpsed water, brown and shineless, sliding by beneath them like the scales of a snake.

"Father will kill us if we get drowned," said Clay, and his steamy breath settled on his lashes like tears.

Crawling at last on hands and knees, resting their hands on their coat cuffs, Clay and Hal reached the ice island where the dog stood bark-bark-barking.

Close to, she looked as big as a horse. When Hal stepped on to her raft of ice, she turned round twice then stood up on her hind paws, the front two on his shoulders, her nose against his. The look in her eyes was pleading. In fact it was almost as sorrowful as their situation.

Icy water washed over their feet. The ice fragment rocked wildly. The crazy paving of the river began to move, the pieces jostling each other for elbow-room. The dog began to lunge to and fro, making things worse. It was like trying to stand teetering on a wet toboggan as it sets off downhill.

"I don't like it here," said Clay (who was, after all, only seven).

"This was your idea," said Hal. He took off his belt and fastened it round the dog as a lead. Her neck was almost the size of his waist. A pathway of water opened up and, with a fearful, gurgling rush, their platform began to slide

4

downstream into the shadow of the Bridge. The dog's barking echoes grew loud under the dark, dripping archway. There was another noise, too: the boys' own voices, calling for help.

"Grab the pillar!" Hal told his little brother. "Time to get off."

Pedestrians curious to see the Great Freeze break up, looked over the bridge parapet. They heard the terrible creaking, grating, crunch and groan of the thawing river. They heard, too, a dog barking and two children's cries for help. Someone fetched a rope and let it down. Hal tied it round his younger brother.

"No!" said Clay. "I won't leave you!"

Hal was touched, until he realised that Clay was talking to the dog. "You go up. The dog can go next."

Up went Clay, scraping his hands and head on pillar and parapet. Hal and the dog crouched on the pier of the

Bridge, huge slabs of ice tumbling by them, faster every moment.

"Catch, boy!" A carrier had stopped his cart on the bank and stood now on the frozen mud, a coil of rope in his hands. Twice, three times he threw it out and Hal failed to catch the end. As it snaked out a third time, Hal reached out, slipped from the stone ledge, and plunged into the river.

The shock was so sharp that he felt nothing: not the cold, not the barging current, not the splash of the dog jumping in after him. He did not even feel the teeth sinking into his collar. Not until his knees grazed the broken bottles and stones of the shore did he realise that he was safe.

The carter hauled him to his feet. "Fool boy."

The dog shook herself, drenching both Hal and the carter with icy Thames water.

2

Hounded Out

The ice-white day had thawed, like the river, into flooding darkness. The shops on London Bridge were closing. Behind upper windows, where the shopkeepers lived, lamps were being lit. Pierre Laguerre, on his way out to buy dinner, banged his front door several times, but it still would not shut. He had one of the houses at the end where the buildings leaned against each other like drunken old men. Nothing in Laguerre's house, from the doorpost to the chimney, stood upright – but then neither did Laguerre. He leaned forwards from the feet, nose jutting out like a rainspout, long hair swinging forwards to meet under his chin.

After another busy day at his easel, Laguerre was hungry.

At the sight of the boys, he threw up his hands. "I saw it!" he cried. "From my window, I saw it! Such daring! Such heroism! I must paint this amazing rescue! You and your dog must model for me! Such a beautiful beast! He is yours?"

"No," said Hal.

"Yes she is! We rescued her!" declared Clay. "She's going to be our dog always! She can guard the shop and sleep on my bed and chase all the rats off the Bridge, and I shall teach her to sit and roll over and fetch a ball and yes, you can paint us, if you please!"

His brother gave him a push that left a wet handprint on Clay's jacket. "If we do not make shift to get indoors," said Hal, "she can have my bed. I shall be dead of cold." He added, after Laguerre was out of earshot, "And we did not rescue her – she rescued *me*."

"That is why Father will love her!" said Clay with perfect confidence.

Hal was not so sure. But just then, he was too cold to think further ahead than a warm fire and a mug of hot milk.

Magog Goggs, their father, was a small man with a large temper. It seemed to spill out of him like stuffing out of an old mattress, so that his cheeks and chin were covered in angry, bristling, red tufts, and his bulgy clothes were all split at the seams. Faced with the dog, he said, "I'll thank you to take that back whence it came, and not a word more about it!"

11

"But Father!" said Hal, without knowing he was going to say it. "This is . . . Gelert! She saved us off the ice. She can guard the shop and protect us from footpads and rebels and foreigners and pirates and pressmen!"

For a moment, Goggs stared at the dog as he might a Persian carpet. He took in her size and the plush splendour of her golden coat, the liquid brown of her eyes and the bushy plume of her tail. Then he said, "Find its owner. It has been fed; it must have an owner. Find its owner and give it back."

The boys' hearts sank within them as if through thawing ice.

They could do nothing until morning: the winter dark allowed the boys to keep 'Gelert' overnight. Even so, their father would not have her in the shop. Hal had to build a lean-to under the steps of the Bridge, using driftwood and rubbish. As he did so, his heart felt as if all the dogs in London had nibbled it; for he had almost come by a dog of his own: nearly and not quite.

Next morning, the brothers picked their way through clutter to the street door. The shop in which they lived – Goggs' Emporium – was so cram-full of miscellaneous goods that just crossing a room was like climbing through a thorn hedge.

Outside the door sat the dog, a piece of coal in her mouth and the shreds of a fishing net caught round a hind paw. Her grin broke the coal. Her tail made a hollow thud on the planking. But there was nothing for it: Gelert must go back to her owner.

Dismal and cold, they walked the streets asking if anyone recognised the dog, knew her owner.

"If we ask no one, no one can claim her," said Clay. "Then we may call her ours!"

But of course such a dog catches the eye and stays in the memory. Before long, a shopkeeper called out to them, "What you be doing with John Hay's dog? Only a butcher could feed such a one!" He sent them in the direction of Chime Alley and the Sign of the Cleaver. The dog, finding herself in familiar streets, grew wildly excited, dashing about, bounding and bouncing with joy.

John Hay was nothing so respectable as a butcher. He was an offal man. He lurked outside a cave of a house, poking at various mounds of kidneys, livers and tripe. His head and hands were peppered with flies. The smell was as thick as breathing porridge.

"Well, blind my eye, you never brought it back!" He greeted the sight of his dog. "After all my pains to be rid of it!" And he slapped his fist down on a quaking mound of tripe.

Clay sank his fingers deep into the

dog's golden fur. "We found her. On the river," he said.

"Where I throwed her, yes," said the offal man.

"You threw your dog off the Bridge?" said Hal in disbelief.

The dog, meanwhile, had begun to lick the ground under the table, the table legs, the stringy danglings of purple offal.

"Do I look like a man with shillings to throw away?" retorted the Offal Man. "Have you not heard? They want two shillings now, before a man can keep a dog."

"Who do?"

"Parliament! The King! The Mayor! How do I know? They passed a law. A two-shilling Dog Tax. Soon as I hear it, I take her down London Bridge and throw her off. If the river hadn't been froze, she mun be in the sea by now and Neptune himself paying the Dog Tax. I know *I* ain't." So saying, he lifted his cleaver off the wall behind him and came around the table. The dog lacked the wit to be afraid. Even though her life was in peril, she went cheerfully on, pouncing after the flies, snuffing up the putrid smell, grinning foolishly and wagging her tail, hypnotised by the liver and lights smoking and reeking on the tabletop.

"Can we have her?" Clay blurted, placing himself between dog and cleaver.

"King himself can have her, for all I

care!" bellowed the Offal Man. Then Clay threw his arms around the man, and Hal threw his arms around the dog who had her head into a bucket of chickens' feet.

"What's her name?" asked Clay, breathless with astonishment that anyone could be so generous. John Hay shrugged. Names were a blessing he had never wasted on animals.

"Dog. I called her Dog," he said, snarling. Hal and Clay did not stay to ask any more.

Laughing out loud, they ran through the streets, down Snows Fields and Newcomen Street and past the Hospital, the dog bounding between them.

"Why did you call her Gelert?" asked Clay.

"Gelert was faithful and true to Prince Llewellyn! To the death!" said Hal.

"Yes, but he was a he, not a she," Clay objected. He might know nothing about reading and writing, but Clay remembered every story Hal had ever told him.

"Grendel, then," said Hal.

"Grendel was a monster!"

"Well? This one's a monstrous big dog."

"Grendel was a monstrous big *monster*," said Clay peevishly. His arm rested tenderly along the dog's long back; her head was on a level with his own. "Anyway. She's ours now. Ours to name. I shall call her . . ."

"I do not think we should speak of the Dog Tax to Father," said Hal. They had reached the door of the house on the Bridge. He need not have worried. Clay, at seven, understood nothing about taxation. All he knew was that he had been given a dog – a huge, golden, friendly dog half as big as a horse, and that life would be perfect for ever more at the Sign of the Golden Hound.

3

The Liability

Magog Goggs' shop was unique on the Bridge in that its goods had price tags, and those prices were fixed. Notices on the wall declared

NO HAGGLING. NO CREDIT.
NO BARTER.

Nothing could be paid for in eggs or salmon. No one was allowed to pay next week or when their luck changed or when business looked up. Goggs was a busy man, and had no time to argue: either customers paid the marked price or they went home empty-handed. But in all his business life, no one had ever offered him something *for free*. The very word "free" so startled him that Hal was able to finish his story without interruption.

"... So the offal man said, Take her! For free! You have her! She's yours. I want no more of her." So now we may have her guard the shop, and run about the town with placards clapped to her sides that say, *Come to Goggs' Emporium at the Sign of the Golden Hound!* and people will come to know the sight of her and say "There's Goggs' hound from that wonderful shop on the Bridge!"

Goggs was secretly terrified of

thieves and gypsies. He suspected all his customers of being light-fingered. A guard dog might be very useful. He liked the idea of the placards too. Fixed Prices had once been a novelty that brought the crowds flocking, but novelty grows stale. Fresh novelties are needed. An advertising dog would soon have the neighbourhood talking again of Goggs' Emporium.

"How is it to be fed?" he asked, puckering up the folds of his face into a look of disgust. "Where will it sleep, just tell me that? Great animal."

But the boys knew they had won.

Other traders on the Bridge had their worries. "Let her but lift her leg against my first editions and she shall never live to do it a second time," said Brooke the bookseller.

"Let her steal a pie from my rack and she shall want for a tail to wag!" said the pieman.

"Let her but frighten my ladies," said the corsetier, "and I shall cut her up for whalebone."

But then their eyes would soften as the big, good-natured dog stood there grinning, and they would reach out a hand and tug her ear or scratch between her eyes or slip her a morsel of bread. They also liked the idea of having their food scraps collected daily by the boys. (They would no longer be put to the trouble of emptying them into the river.)

That night, Magog Goggs allowed himself a trip to the Flying Horse for a glass of porter, leaving the boys collecting scraps from the neighbours and the shop guarded by the dog. In fact, Goggs' hopes were high. He bought a second porter and began to talk loudly about his plans for a new shop sign – a golden hound – and of stocking parrots and caged canaries.

The man beside him at the counter

wore the livery of a royal swan-upper, and had spent the day counting dead swans on the river: swans killed by the bitter weather. "You must be turning a fine profit these days, Goggs, if you can afford to keep a dog," he said. "I had to turn mine out of doors when the Tax came in."

Magog explained his excellent plan for feeding the dog cheaply on household rubbish.

"Yes, but what of the Dog Tax?" said the swan-upper. "If I had a florin to spare, I would sooner take in a new pair of boots than a wolfhound half as big as the parlour."

Magog Goggs took a swig of his ale. Around him, other drinkers began to nod dolefully. "Had a pair of terriers mysel'," said O'Connell. "Match and Powder. Neatest little pups you ever saw. But how's a man to find four shillings, eh? I walked them to Hampstead Heath and turned them loose." He mopped his eyes with a handkerchief, sad to be reminded of his doglessness.

Magog Goggs took another sup of his drink.

"You and a thousand like you," said the tapster of the Flying Horse. "I hear the strays are forming up into wild packs – dragging riders from their horses. Madness I call it, a tax that fills the streets with homeless, hungry dogs! Madness!"

Magog Goggs twisted his empty glass round and round on the counter, staring into it as though into a crystal ball. "The . . . er . . . Dog Tax . . . ?" he said.

The customers of the Flying Horse were in perfect agreement: no government ought to tax the owning of dogs. It was all very well for the gentry with their spotted talbot-hounds and their hunting packs . . . How were common folk supposed to afford *two shillings*? And why should they have to do without the companionship of a faithful pet? It was a bitter shame.

"I threw my Sally into the canal in a sack," said a coalman.

"I knocked mine on the head," said a plumber.

By the time Magog Goggs left the inn, a dozen grown men were weeping into their ale, remembering the dogs they had been forced to part with.

Goggs was almost weeping, too. To think he had been about to advertise the fact that he owned a dog! There was no time to be lost. He must get rid of the brute before the taxman came calling for his two shillings! How had the news passed him by? It seemed that all London knew of the Dog Tax, but not Goggs!

This was no wonder, of course. The world is divided into those who own

dogs, and those who do not. Magog
Goggs had simply never taken an
interest in dogs before today. Even so, he
cursed his sons. Why, they had almost
cost him a silver florin with their stupid
notion of keeping a dog . . . "They'll be
taxing us next for having children – or
wives! – or clotheshorses!" he fumed on
his walk home. "Placards, indeed! For
two shilling I could hire the Town Crier!
Do those boys think I am quilted out
with money? Pay two shillings to keep a
dog?"

When he was still a furlong from
his shop, Goggs began to hear an
unfamiliar noise. It was of chinking china
and tinkling metal, loud thumps and soft
thuds. There was a rattling cascade and
some explosive coughing. He quickened
his pace. A little crowd of passers-by had
gathered in front of the shop: one was
trying to peer in at the window.

"What's astir, Goggs?" asked his

neighbour, the tobacconist. Goggs fumbled with his keys.

Left alone in the shop, the Golden Hound had begun to explore. Perhaps she was looking for a name among the powder boxes and mugs; the fishing floats and mousetraps, the flat irons and picture frames. Somehow a basket of billiard balls got overturned on the landing; as Goggs opened the door, they came bouncing down the stairs towards him. So did the dog. A skein of knitting wool was tangled round her legs. She must have walked through the puddle of spilled ink, too, because there were scarlet paw prints on the wall. A stuffed stool appeared to have put up a brave struggle, fleeing around the room before losing the fight and all its horsehair stuffing. A coach lamp lay broken in the hearth, and the biscuit barrels were full of sand from the spilled fire bucket. At first sight, Goggs thought the dog had

eaten a customer, leaving only the bones. But on closer inspection it proved to be his tray of clay pipes scattered across the floor. A snow of price labels had settled over the whole unhappy scene.

When Goggs hit her with the empty fire bucket, the Golden Hound bit him on the ankle.

Hal and Clay got home, their hands full of fish-heads and chop bones, to find there had been a certain . . . change of mood since teatime. The Golden Hound was no longer a prized member of the family. In fact, Goggs was chasing her around the shop with the poker, roaring oaths and asking to know why anyone would pay two shillings to save such a dog from the gallows.

4

A Fair Likeness

"Take it out and lose it!" That was what their father had said. But these things are not so simple. Hal and Clay took the Golden Hound as far as London Fields, Clay crying every step of the way, and left her under a tree.

"Sit. Stay," they told her. She jumped up and licked Hal's face.

"Sit. Stay," they said, and she rolled on to her back and offered her golden stomach to be scratched.

Hal threw a stick. But the offal man had never played with his dog. So before they could desert her, they had to first teach her the trick of fetching a stick. Finally, Hal hurled it as far as his twiggy arms would let him, and while she ran to fetch it, they betrayed her by running as fast as they could in the opposite direction.

They ran till the houses closed in around them. They ran till the tears dried on their cheeks. They outran their own breath.

"We could have called her Eldorado!" panted Clay at last. "Or Gilda!"

"She trusted us," said Hal.

"*Arff*," said the Golden Hound, bouncing round them with the stick in her mouth and undimmed love in her eyes.

So they tied her to a lamppost in Blackwall and moved away by easy stages, telling each other she would be found, she would be freed, she would be loved and fed and given a home.

"Or else she may starve," said Clay.

"Or pine for us," said Hal.

"Or freeze in the middle of the night," whimpered Clay.

"*Arff*," said the Golden Hound, who had chewed through the rope and come trotting after them. (She had probably followed the trail of tear-splashes along the pavement.)

"Father will skin us alive if we take her home," said Hal.

"Ah well. I like her better than Father anyway," said Clay. "Let's run away."

Hal preferred to be sensible; after all, he was nine and old enough to know better than Clay. There again he, too, liked the dog better than his father just then. "We shall not take her home!" he said, one finger raised in inspiration, ". . . Leastway, not till we have earned the money to PAY THE TAX!"

Laguerre was the son of a French artist who had decorated the salons of a dozen noble houses. Pierre had learned his trade at his father's knee, and become a painter himself almost without thinking. In fact thinking was not something Pierre Laguerre did much of. He was a man of impulse. If he saw a view that pleased him, he painted it. If he had an impulse to sleep, he slept. If he felt the pangs of hunger, he ate. If someone knocked at the door and he was in the mood for company, he opened up.

"You said you wished to paint the Rescue!" gabbled the boy on his threshold. "Here we are. Here is the dog."

"You said we should come," said

Clay, in case Laguerre had missed the point. "Our fee is two shillings!"

"And the dog must stop here till it is done!" added Hal.

Both boys ducked their heads inside their collars, for fear Laguerre would swat them off his doorstep.

"Good! Excellent! Come in!" The artist was delighted to see them, drawing them inside, offering them glasses of hot wine, moving pots of turpentine so that they could sit down. The floor underfoot was tacky with a dozen colours of oil paint. On various tables stood dead fruit, a vase of dead flowers, the bust of a Roman goddess: subjects Laguerre had started to paint at some time or another. The canvas on the easel at present, though, had no more on it than a few watery lines. He sponged these off at once, declaring he would paint the heroic Rescue and that it would make him famous.

Hal was fearful he might have to re-enact the dreadful day of the thaw, and balance on the footings of the Bridge again, or plunge into the river. Fortunately Laguerre never painted out of doors. As he told them, "Too uncomfortable, Master Goggs. A man might catch his death *en plein air.*"

No, Laguerre preferred to paint indoors – whenever the light was right, the mood was on him and it was not a mealtime.

He draped the boys over the dog like washing over a clothesline and eyed them over the edge of his thumbs. The dog proved to be a wonderful artist's model. She was content to sit like a lion on a monument, her soft jowls spread on Hal's shoulder. Only her paws twitched sometimes when she fell asleep and dreamt of rabbits or offal.

The boys, on the other hand, found it hard to sit still for more than two

minutes without needing to scratch or stretch or giggle or use the water closet. They had time to rename the dog over and over again. (They settled at last on "Gloria".) Modelling was very, very dull.

Alongside Laguerre, though, they were patience itself. He no sooner took up a brush than he needed to mix more colour – or light a pipe – or read them a piece from the newspaper – or pop out for a cup of chocolate. He would practise the flute, or shop for liquorice or change his shoes or trim his pointed beard. Sometimes he was just not in the mood to paint. He said his "muse" was sleeping. Laguerre liked to sleep, too, especially after a meal.

The winter freeze had made the houses at this end of the Bridge lean even more drunkenly. Laguerre had a big bow window that jutted out over the river, and when the tide was high, the whole building groaned like a thing in pain. The windows allowed a lot of grimy light to pour into the room like lemon juice filling a jar. It also let in a biting draught where the frame was splitting away from the wall. Hal and Clay quickly found this out, since this was where Laguerre sat them while he prepared to paint "The Rescue".

Hal eyed the gap between window and wall, and the water below it. "Do you ever fear to fall in the river, Mr Laguerre?" he asked.

"All the time, all the time, *mon cher copain*! But one cannot give in to fear! What would life be if we gave in to our fears? . . . Shall we peel an apple and read the future?"

So Laguerre went out and bought a pound of apples and, one by one, they peeled them and threw the peel over their shoulders. If the fallen peel looked like a letter, they would instantly know the first letter of their true love's name.

Unfortunately, as fast as they threw the peel, the Golden Hound ate it, so they ended up just as unsure of the future as when they began.

A big sailing barge squeezed under the centre arches of the Bridge; they heard it bang and scrape against the pilings. The house shuddered like a dog.

Every evening, while their father was at the Flying Horse, Hal and Clay went along the Bridge to the artist's house and posed for the picture that would bring them their two-shilling fee. The Golden Hound remained with Laguerre, leading a secret life. As far as Magog Goggs was concerned, the dog had been left on London Fields: one more victim of the Dog Tax.

One month passed, and then two. Rosebay willowherb appeared on the roofs of London. But the canvas on Laguerre's easel was still as white as winter. Maybe soon the background would be filled in, the stonework painted, and the figures in the foreground finished . . .

Hal and Clay did not dare to press for their fee, though they longed to present it to their father:

"Here you are, Father! Two shillings to pay the Dog Tax! And here is the kennel we have made for her. We would show you her portrait, too, but the King has bought it, to hang in Windsor Castle!"

Clay hated to leave the Hound each evening and pick himself clean of dog hairs so that his father would not suspect. One evening at supper he suddenly and unthinkingly said, "Do you think she misses us?"

"Who?" said Goggs, through a mouthful of fruit.

It was an awkward moment. Clay crammed food into his mouth so as not to have to reply.

"That lovely old dog we rescued from the river," said Hal. "We think of her. Sometimes."

"Herumph," said Goggs, and spat a cherry stone at the wall.

Laguerre had a wig of long black curls that hung luxuriantly round the shoulders of a purple velvet frock-coat. But he did not seem to have any second wig, any second jacket. He did not appear to have a roomful of finished paintings for sale or any food on the shelves. He was never gone long on his supper trips, and his breath afterwards never smelled of anything but sack wine. The furniture seemed to be stealing away, too, as if it feared for its life in the rickety house on the Bridge.

With every day that passed, Laguerre looked more and more uneasy. In the last week of March, he worked more on "The Rescue" than he had done in the ten weeks before. The bridge in the picture grew solid; beneath it a frozen Thames, above it a sky green with unshed snow. The painted parapets wept icicles.

This time, when Laguerre went out for his supper, Hal and Clay crept from the window seat to stare in wonder at the picture. The very sight of it made them shiver. Two boys and a dog clung to the footings of the Bridge, while rescuers clustered above them and along the shoreline.

"It is very fine," said Hal.

"The King is sure to buy it," said Clay. "Is it finished, do you suppose?"

"There is no canvas showing."

"Does that mean we get our florin?"

Hal bit his lip. "I'll ask. Tonight! I shall!"

From outside came the noise of shouting. The door flew open and

Laguerre tumbled in, wig in hand. He slammed shut the door.

"Look out, *copains*! The bailiffs are on me!" He took the picture from the easel and threw it to them. He picked up his flute and dropped it down one trouser leg. Then he reached for his brushes.

The lock on the door burst, and two men shouldered their way inside. In the small room, and wearing their dogskin coats, they seemed as big as bears and just as ferocious. They picked up the stool as if it were a sheep ready for slaughter. They picked up the chairs and the fire tongs. They threw open the cupboard doors and stuck in their heads, looking for any pot of jam, any nutmeg, any twist of tobacco that could be sold. They took the bowl that had held the apples, and the easel that had held the picture.

"What are you doing here?" they demanded of Hal.

"He owes us two shillings!" said Hal. "We came here to ask for it."

"Join the queue!" scoffed the bailiff. "This one has more debts than a dog has fleas. Is that his dog?"

"No! It's ours," cried Clay and flung his arms round the dog's neck.

They searched Laguerre and found his flute. They confiscated a roll of new canvas and the palette still wet with paint. They took up the rug and pulled down the curtains. They even confiscated the shop-sign of pallet and brushes from over the street door.

Then they were gone, and Laguerre, too – dragged away to debtors' prison without tools or materials to paint his way out of debt.

The boys crouched as still as if the bailiffs had taken the very house and left them adrift on the Thames below it. Outside, the noise of their trundling handcart and Laguerre's loud protests moved away along the Bridge.

"Give me time to sell some work!"
Laguerre was pleading. *"I have had
expenses! I have had that dog of theirs
to feed!"*

Hal got slowly to his feet. So did
Clay.

"Stand up, girl," they told the
Hound, and she raised her golden flanks
off the picture she had been hiding from
the bailiffs.

"We never got our two shillings,"
said Clay.

"We must get it some other way,"
said Hal, keeping his voice as level as
possible; he could see that his little
brother had been seriously scared by the
roughness of the bailiffs.

"We could sell the painting," said
Clay. "It must be worth two shillings!"

"It is not ours to sell," said Hal.
"But we should hide it somewhere while
we are away."

"Away?" cheeped Clay.

"Away, earning the Dog Tax," said Hal decisively. "In the country."

5

Eating Crow

Throughout the land, families with dogs were facing the same dilemma. The shepherd with his collie, the whirligig player with his dancing dog, many found that they must either be rid of their animal or go without eating. Those who scraped together the tax money for a well-loved bitch found they must drown her puppies for fear they receive a demand for a guinea more.

The rich, of course, were happy to pay. Strings of ghost-coloured greyhounds followed behind liveried carriages like a wake behind a ship. Lapdogs howled their way through concerts and operas. Valets in scarlet livery were towed about the public parks by Irish wolfhounds.

But inns called The Talbot and The Greyhound never saw a dog in their yards now. For the ordinary man, two shillings was just too great a price to pay for the joy of a wire-haired or curly-coated companion. In villages, cities and farmland, dogs were turned out of doors, pelted with stones to drive them away from their old haunts. In the forests and fields the squirrels and rabbits found they had a new breed of foe – the hungry, homeless dog forced to fend for itself.

Hal and Clay knew just how these outcasts felt. They could not go home either – not if they were to keep Gloria. And so these two boys, who had never set foot outside the City of London, found themselves traipsing through April rain on muddy April roads between hedges of may blossom and hawthorn.

They found themselves work on a farm. At least, Gloria found them work. Seeing a flock of crows settle on to a newly-planted field, she went pouncing after them like a kitten chasing butterflies. When the farmer popped up from behind a hedge, Hal thought he would be angry to see the dog trespassing.

"I'm sorry. I'll fetch her," he said, starting to climb over the gate of the field.

"Leave her be," said the farmer. "Crows are sent by the Devil to plague a farming man."

So all three stood at the gate and watching Gloria give the crows the greatest scare of their lives. They got talking, and Hal explained their journey in search of two shillings to pay the Dog Tax.

"A penny a day to keep the crows away," said the Farmer.

For a moment, Hal thought it was one of those wise old country sayings. After a moment, he realised it was an offer of work. Twelve pennies, one shilling. Twenty-four days and they would earn enough to pay the Dog Tax.

"It is a bargain, sir!" said Hal. He spat on to his palm and held it out. (He was sure that was how things were down in the country.) Farmer Jellicoe looked at the palm with disgust and put his hands behind his back. "You keep your dirty town ways to yourself, boy," he said. "You may sleep in the barn."

* * *

Each day, Farmer Jellicoe's steward toured the fields on a pony, his feet trailing along the ground and behind him a pannier of bread and cheese. There was a flagon of cider, too. The sowers each owned a tin mug to hold their daily ration of cider. Hal and Clay had to make do with a slurp from the flagon. But they were given a chunk of bread and a lump of cheese, and an apple.

The Golden Hound ate crow.

Hal and Clay had little to do but sit and watch the dog earn their wages. But when she slumped down to sleep, they had to take her place, throwing stones and whirling their jackets at the thieving birds. The crows, it seemed, had made it their life's work to eat the farmer's seed. Fortunately, the Golden Hound had made it her crusade to stop them.

Once, a man stopped his cart as he drove by the field where they sat. He, too, watched the Golden Hound pouncing to and fro. As he watched, he fingered his half moustache. The man was half-shaven from the crown of his half-bald head to the tip of his half-bearded jaw. Along the inside of his cart hung a row of glistening knives on a length of washline.

"I'll give you two shillings," he said.

It seemed like a wish granted by the fairies. Clay rose on to the scuffed toes of his boots and began to bounce up and down, tugging on his brother's sleeve.

"What for? For what will you give us two shillings, sir?" said Hal.

"For the dog, of course. For her outsides, anyhow. Let me introduce myself: Skinner Hackett's the name. Skinning's my trade."

"She's not for sale, sir," said Hal, trying to keep his voice calm, despite the horror boiling up inside him.

"I can understand that. Fine dog," said Skinner Hackett. "A boy can grow fond of such a dog. Active. Spry." His eyes, as he looked the dog over, moved from joint to joint, like a butcher planning how to joint a carcass of meat. "E'en so. All flesh is grass. What when her days are done, eh? When the candle is out? In short . . . when she is dead?"

Clay, only dimly understanding, looked up into his brother's face for reassurance. "We'll bury Gloria in her skin, shan't we, Hal?"

"No sale," said Hal, choking down his disgust.

"Are you sure?" said Hackett. "Shall we put things to the test?"

Reaching behind him, Hackett took down a muzzle-loading pistol and a fleshing knife.

"No sale, I said!" squeaked Hal. But Skinner Hackett did not seem to have heard him, because he proceeded to load the pistol, laboriously tipping powder down the barrel and tamping it home with a thin rod. When he had added the ball, he took careful aim. The dog, who had just felled a crow, was preparing to eat it for lunch. Skinner Hackett aimed at her head.

"Gloria! Look out! NO!" yelled Clay.

There was a flash and a noise like a cat spitting, then a bang that made the Hound dance up on to her hind paws.

Skinner Hackett examined the pistol and frowned. "Shoddy foreign goods," he said peevishly. "Another flash in the pan." He seemed almost to expect their sympathy. Whistling tunelessly, he began to reload the Switzer.

Hal took hold of his brother's collar, and ran, calling Gloria to follow. They ran and they ran, expecting any minute a bang from the gun and the heat of a bullet in the back. Reaching a spinney of trees, they twisted their bodies round behind the trunks of the trees, trying to persuade the dog, too, to make herself spindle-thin behind a birch tree.

From their hiding place, they saw the skinner shrug and hang up the tools of his trade. Without any sign of anger or irritation, he picked up the reins and shouted at his horse to "move it along, you old bag of bones!" and the cart clip-clopped away along the road.

Within three weeks, the field where they had first met Farmer Jellicoe began to green over like a pond in spring. The ploughboys and sowers had finished scattering their seedcorn. The crop was underground and sprouting. Gloria's big paws began to do more damage to the young plants than the crows or seagulls.

"Twenty-four days," said Jellicoe's steward, and instead of their bread and

cheese, handed them the caps they had
left in the barn overnight. "Safe journey
to you."

"May we have our two shillings,
sir?" said Hal. Excitement tinged his
voice at the thought of all those big
pennies and bright thruppences.

"Best call at the farmhouse if you
are after being paid."

Jellicoe was eating a cold pie and pickle,
when they knocked at the door. The
housekeeper said he had company and
could not be disturbed, but he emerged
into the hall and waved her aside. They
tried to leave their dog outside the door,
but Gloria seemed to think she was about
to be paid too. Leading them back into
his parlour, Jellicoe took down a coffee
caddy from the mantelpiece. "Twenty-
four pennies I promised you and here
they are," he said, and laid them out on
the long, pine table.

Hal put his upturned cap by the
table-edge, ready to sweep them in.

"One moment!" said Farmer
Jellicoe. "There are your expenses,
remember."

"Expenses?"

"Well, there's the half-pence a day
for lodging . . ." Jellicoe picked up
twelve of the coins. "There's one farthing
a day for lunch . . ." He picked up
another six. "A penny for the damage

done by your dog to my young crop . . .
And shall we say thruppence for kennel
fees? That leaves, I believe, one penny
each." And he presented the pennies as
if he were awarding medals in a time of
war.

Open-mouthed but speechless, Hal
and Clay reached out to take their
solitary pennies.

". . . And that will do for my
tutoring fees!" laughed Jellicoe,
snatching the pennies away.

"Your . . ."

"For teaching you mathematics!"

Hal looked beyond the farmer to
his housekeeper, appealing for justice,
but the housekeeper only broke out
laughing at the Master's cleverness.
Someone else in the room also barked
with laughter; Jellicoe's lunch
companion stood up out of the wing
chair by the fireside.

"Now, if you will permit me to

advise you," Jellicoe was saying as he replaced the caddy on the mantelpiece, "you'll strike a deal with my friend here. He has money to spend and you have something he wishes to buy."

They had not seen the "friend's" face while he sat in the chair, but now there was no mistaking it. It was Skinner Hackett.

Once Skinner Hackett saw an exceptional pelt, he did not take no for an answer. Why, on one occasion he had trailed a spotted talbot all the way across Kent to its home. The talbot's owner had not wanted to sell either, but after his dog mysteriously died overnight, he had been glad enough to take five shillings for the body. This golden giant was definitely something special – something worth a little extra trouble. In fact, Skinner would have paid twice two shillings for its skin: its sheer size would make four waistcoats or one roomy winter coat for the largest of his clients.

And now he would not have to pay a penny. Jellicoe would willingly swear that five bright shillings had changed hands in his kitchen. Who would believe a couple of London boys who said any different?

His pistol was primed and ready. He hated to use the Switzer – it made a hole in the pelt – but already Hackett had more bites in him than the coastline of Norway and he did not like to get bitten, especially by a dog as big as this one.

"I am obliged to you, friend Jellicoe," he said, and took careful aim at the Golden Hound.

6

Running Wild

Then Hal did something extraordinarily
foolish. He sprang forward, snatched the
gun out of Hackett's hand, and threw it
as far as his strength would let him.
Hackett let fly with his fists and a curse.
The dog looked up and saw the pistol
arc through the parlour door, skid along
the quarry-tiled passage and thud into a

pile of muddy boots lying by the door.

She was there.

The boys had taught her to fetch, and fetch she did, lifting aside the boots with her big paws, folding her soft mouth around the metal (though the smell of it was sharp as pepper). She came trotting back with the pistol and laid it down in the centre of the parlour floor, waiting for words of praise.

For a moment everyone stared at the Switzer. Then it was back in Skinner Hackett's palm, slippery with dog spit but still cocked and ready to fire. He gave a jackal's grin and fired – felt the sharp recoil and laughed. No flash in the pan this time. This time he had . . .

He had no time to think anything more before the dog landed on his chest and knocked him to the floor.

"That's it! Kill him! Kill him!" Clay yelled, sobbing with fright and anger.

The Golden Hound, though, was

not a vengeful dog: she did not bear
grudges – not against the Offal Man who
had thrown her off London Bridge, not
against the Farmer who had stolen her
hard labour, not against the Skinner who
made ear-splitting noises with his little
handful of metal. No, Gloria was
interested only in Skinner's fur waistcoat:
the one that smelled of greyhound and
spaniel and sweat and cordite and
mutton gravy and tobacco. She stood on
Hackett's chest and thrust her nose into
each of his pockets in turn. It was as if
you or I were to stick our heads into the
hold of a ship laden with exotic spices.

Hal picked up the Switzer and
threw it into the stove. Clay picked up
the fleshing knife and threw it out of the
window. The Golden Hound gave one
last lick to the skinner's face and
followed them, running down the drive.

You may wonder why the farmer
did nothing to stop them. But since the

dog's jaws had bent the pistol's barrel . . .

. . . and since the bullet had swerved and struck Jellicoe square in the chest . . .

. . . there was nothing much he could do but lie on his back, looking at his parlour ceiling with eyes as glazed as a dead herring's.

Behind them, as they ran, Hal and Clay heard the housekeeper scream and Skinner Hackett start to shout: *"I didn't do it! I was aiming at the dog! Ask the brats! I was aiming at the dog! Tell her Jellicoe! I was aiming at the dog!"*

They did not stop running until they were deep inside Epping Forest and hopelessly lost. The late afternoon did not dare to follow them in among the trees, and they found themselves in an alien gloom where only tall tree trunks held off the sky, and where the undergrowth rattled with unseen life.

They slept with their dog for a pillow and nothing in their stomachs. They woke damp through and as tired as ever, exhausted by dreams of wolves and ghosts and pistols. Nor did the dreams melt away in the dawn. They stuck, like wet clothes, and would not be peeled off.

There *were* animals crashing about unseen. There *were* howls and barks and dark shapes moving among the ferns. Shadowy runners kept pace with them as they picked their way along yet another path, only to find it led nowhere and they had to retrace their steps. Not one but thirty pairs of eyes watched them climb a tree in the hope of spying a road or a house. And what did they see when they had managed it at last? Nothing but a sea of green leaves.

That was when the dogs showed themselves.

Below them, Gloria started up an odd, muted barking. They peered between the branches to see her crouched flat, tail tucked under, ears down. Then, into the clearing came thirty or forty dogs – a motley troupe of breeds with just one thing in common: they were running wild.

These were the dogs who had been turned out of doors by owners unable to pay the Dog Tax. These were dogs who had given unquestioning love to man, woman or child, only to find themselves friendless and hungry. Alone and bewildered, they had wandered through markets, suburbs and farms, joining forces with other dogs in the same plight. Pairs had formed into gangs, gangs into packs. The warmth of other flanks, the racket of barking, the welter of doggy smells stirred up ancient instincts. These outcasts were part of a pack and a pack has no need of people – except as prey.

"I did not know that dogs lived in forests," whispered Clay.

"They have nowhere else to live," Hal explained. "They are strays who have joined up into groups. For company." He did not want to frighten his little brother.

"Will they eat Gloria?" said Clay, who did not need his brother's help to be frightened. "Or will Gloria join up with them and eat us?"

Hal made a snorting noise. "How can they eat us? We are up a tree. Now be quiet."

Closer and closer the strays ringed Gloria round. She pressed herself so close to the bracken that she seemed half buried. A terrier ran in and snapped at her flank. A spaniel bounced on to her spine and off again. Still, the pack was wary of her, because of her great size. As for the boys in the tree – well, they would have to come down sooner or later, and then they would be easy meat.

Suddenly something happened that

made the pack forget both the giant golden dog and the boys overhead.

Though unable to see it, Hal and Clay had in fact come within a stone's throw of a broad forest track. Along it now came a two-wheeled trap pulled by a tiny, snow-white pony. The driver – a woman in sky blue velvet – had not stumbled into the forest by accident. She had not slept among the ferns nor breakfasted on air. The Dog Tax had caused her no hardship. In fact hardship was as unknown to Lady Holland as Epping Forest was to the Goggs boys. But no one had warned her about the gangs of stray dogs roaming the Forest. (Or if they had, she had been too obstinate to listen.) When the pack came bounding towards her, she was momentarily charmed by the little white terrier, the curly-coated springer, the scruffy mutt who came leaping over the fallen trees.

Her horse was quicker to see the danger. It bolted, caught one wheel on a big tree root, and turned the cart over on its side. Half the pack encircled the fallen pony; the other half encircled the woman where she lay among the rotting acorns of the old year.

Only when the biggest dog of all arrived did Lady Holland find the power to scream.

Gloria was a sociable dog. She liked the company of other dogs. Seeing the

pack turn its back on her, she naturally went after it, calling out to the other dogs in her huge throaty voice. Finding the dogs arrayed in a frozen crouch around the wreckage of a cart, she knocked each one down playfully, to find out which wanted to wrestle with her.

The driver picked up her driving whip and began to crack it. Between the cracking of the whip, and the pouncing of the enormous golden dog, the heart went out of the pack; they were little lost dogs again, fleeing through the trees, scratching themselves on the brambles. Gloria went after them but was side-tracked by her first sight of a squirrel. By the time she had chased the squirrel and lost it, all the wild dogs were gone. Glumly she traipsed back towards the clearing, before she lost the boys, as well.

Lady Holland was still crouched behind her flimsy pony cart when Clay came into sight. He had hurled himself out of the tree, thinking his beautiful dog was deserting him to join the pack. Now he came running through the trees yelling, *"Do not go, Gloria! Abide here with us! We love you!"*

His brother had no option but to chase after Clay or see him torn to pieces by wild dogs. So he too came pelting through the forest, one shoe gone, one sleeve snagged out of his jacket. The little white pony wagged its stubby legs in the air and showed the whites of its eyes.

It came as a pleasant surprise to everyone to find that Gloria had saved the day. No one was more surprised than Gloria.

7

Just Rewards

Lady Holland expressed her thanks as
only a lady can. She touched Clay's
cheek, presented a gloved hand to Hal,
and flung her arms around Gloria.
"Thank you! Oh thank you! Thank you!
Thank you! By the grace of God, you
saved my life!"

Together, Hal and Clay freed the

pony from its traces, righted the cart, then ran behind it as Lady Holland bowled out of the Forest.

Gradually, the trees grew sparser. Grass took the place of bracken. The tall, Tudor chimneys of a tall, Tudor house came into sight, and then a driveway and a valley-full of formal gardens. Iron gates shut with a clang behind them, shutting out the wild dogs of Epping.

"I am greatly indebted to you, young man," said Lady Holland later, and Hal's ears burned red at the rim. "Would I insult you very much if I were to offer you some small reward?"

"Two shillings would not insult us!" Clay blurted out, so loud that Hal clapped a hand over his mouth and apologised. Then he explained all about Gloria and the Dog Tax. Over luncheon, Lady Holland listened to the whole story, gasping and sighing so often that they began to think she was making fun of them. "But your poor father! He must be so anxious for your safety!" she said at last.

"We left a note," said Clay, his mouth crammed with cold chicken.

"Even so! You must hasten home and set his mind at rest! You shall have your two shillings – and your fare home to London."

And so, after six hours of skating on the Thames, after six weeks of sitting still for Pierre Laguerre, after twenty-four days of chasing crows, after a nightmare night in Epping Forest, the Golden Hound finally earned herself the price of belonging.

Next day, when the Ongar stage-driver refused to carry a large yellow dog – "*She may be a heroine but what will she do to my upholstery?*" – Lady Holland told her own coachman to prepare a carriage and carry her guests home to London.

"Would that I had a portrait of this

lovely dog!" she said, standing on the running board to fondle Gloria's ears. "My husband will scarce believe me when he returns home!"

"You should buy Mr Laguerre's picture," said Clay shamelessly. "The one of The Rescue!"

Lady Holland had stepped down, and the carriage was drawing away at a smart trot. "Is a good painting?" she called after them.

"Good as any Leonardo de Angelo!" called Hal, standing up, hand cupped round his mouth.

"Then send it to me and it shall settle your friend's debts!"

The boys kept picturing Laguerre's face as he stepped clear of prison, a free man, his debts all paid from the proceeds of the painting. They pictured, too, the scene as their coach drew up outside the shop on the Bridge. How the neighbours would stare as they climbed down, followed by their heroic Golden Hound! Their father would rush forwards: "Where have you been, dear boys? Oh come to my arms! How I regret my churlishness! How glad I am to see you, all three, safe and well!"

Actually, the last part was a little hard to imagine, but Clay and Hal refused to worry. They had come by the money for the Dog Tax, and now they were escaping the murderous countryside for the safety of London, their dog by their side and their sights set on saving Laguerre.

What with their night in the forest, their big lunch, and the rolling of the coach, they were asleep before they had passed Chingford. They slept dreamlessly on through the greatest treat of their lives, until they were woken by the driver shouting out for directions:

". . . missed my turn. Does the Bridge not lie this way?" The carriage had come to a standstill.

"... closed ... order of the Commissioners ... falling down ..." came the reply.

Hal looked out on the familiar riverside buildings, the gleam of the river, the early evening lamplight.

"I fear I can take you and your ... *animal* no farther," said the driver. (His tone said he should never have been asked to take them farther than the garden gate.) "London Bridge is closed."

"Why? Why is it closed?" Clay was bleary with sleep.

The driver delivered the bad news as if on a silver salver. "Because the houses upon it are being torn down."

At the entrance to the Bridge, a man had been posted to keep people from crossing. But Clay and Hal, who had lived on the Bridge all their lives, had no difficulty in getting past him to the shop

– what was left of it, at least.

Masonry was strewn over the road surface, where grappling hooks had been used to claw the houses down. Unwanted belongings lay among the bricks: boxes and baskets and mildewed old bottles; doormats and rags of faded curtain; tuffets and tables without their full quota of legs. What had become of their owners? Where was the hat-maker and the jeweller, the butcher or the will-maker?

It was like arriving home after the End of the World and finding everyone else had been taken up to Heaven.

The Goggs' shop stood roofless, its walls reduced to a broken shell. It was the shape of a sandcastle after the tide has washed over it. Tears welling in their eyes, Hal and Clay searched among the piles of bricks. They half expected to find their father among the rubble. All they found was one of his old gloves. They set it down in front of the dog. "Smell, Gloria! Seek! Scent him out! There's a good girl!"

Gloria squinted down her nose at the glove, flopped down on to her stomach . . . and ate it: fingers, palm and lining.

"Oh Gloria, how could you!" wailed Clay. "Now we shall never find Father again!"

8

Hangdog Homecoming

"Hoi! You boys! Stand where you are!"

The Night Watch, shapeless and rustling in their gabardine capes, advanced on the boys with menace. Hal and Clay made no attempt to move. "Looting, is it? Picking over the bones?"

"What happened?" was all Hal

said. "What befell the shop? Where is Goggs' Emporium?"

The Leader of the Watch held up a lantern and studied the boys' faces. "You have been forth out of London," he said more gently. "It was decided last month – to tear down the houses on the Bridge before they fell down of their own accord. They shall be rebuilt, never fear. Is it Goggs you are looking for? He has temporary premises in Chain Alley – by the Flying Horse. You get yourself thence – or must I run you in for defying City Orders and entering on to the Bridge?"

"I hate the Government," said Clay defiantly. "They tax dogs and pull down people's houses!" Hal hustled him hastily away.

The house in Chain Alley was unlit, but common sense came to their aid. "He will be in the Flying Horse," said Hal, and of course Goggs was. But as they stood outside the inn, they could not help wondering what kind of welcome they would get. How worried Goggs must have been about them! How angry he might be, despite his joy at seeing them safe and well.

Their father's smile, as they pushed indoors, laid all their fears to rest. The lamp-lit features broke into a grin as broad as the Strand, and Goggs flung wide his arms, slopping ale out of the mug in his hand. "Speak of the Devil and he shall appear!" exclaimed Goggs. "See! The wanderers have returned! And look! They have brought that grand dog with them!"

"Ah. Yes," said Hal with a nervous grin (and some surprise; he had thought Gloria was tied up in the street outside). "But we can pay for her now, Father! We have been working to earn the two shillings. That is where we have been – earning the Dog Tax."

"And we came all the way home in

a lady's covered coach – with springs!"
Clay piped up. "Give him the florin, Hal!
Give Father our florin!"

Goggs looked at the silver coin
shining in the palm of his hand, and his
eyes glittered. He had been drinking for
a good long while; he had to keep
moving his feet to keep his balance.
"Well then. Well then. A drink for all my
friends!" he said and clicked the coin
down on the bar.

"Drink up, friends," said the
tapster. "Goggs' ship has just come in."

"But Father . . ." Clay began.

Goggs held up a podgy hand. "Do
not fret yourself, boy. I can afford to be
generous! If you will only find me a coil
of good, strong rope, we shall, without
delay, earn us five shillings more!" And
he jabbed the stem of his pipe at the
public notices tacked to a pillar in the
centre of the room. The largest notice
read:

> **Ready money**
> Those persons who will hang
> their dogs and
> bring the skins to the Flying Horse,
> Monday next, shall receive for every
> skin not less than 3 shillings.
> Large dogs 5 shillings.
> Skins to be clean taken off
> and without slits.

Magog Goggs began piling the furniture up, stool upon bench upon table, creating a wooden mountain at the heart of the bar-room. His drunken friends joined in, anxious to share in Goggs' good fortune. No one could find any rope, but someone fetched a long, leather coaching rein. Then twelve gentlemen at least set about the sport of lynching the Golden Hound.

Five times they chased her around the room, while the tapster shouted for order and Hal threw furniture in their path and Clay wept open-mouthed. Somehow a noose was fashioned from the rein and the rest of the leather thrown over a ceiling beam. A drayman from the brewery scooped up Gloria in both arms but, burdened with the wriggling dog, found it impossible to climb on to the beer-slimy bench. The noose was round the prisoner's neck, but no one could lift her on to the scaffold to hang her.

"A pie! Give me a pie!" cried Goggs. A stale pasty was placed on the topmost chair.

"Fetch! Up!" cried Goggs.

"No! Don't, Gloria! Leave it!" shouted Hal.

Naturally, Gloria saw the pie and instantly leapt on to the table, scrabbling ungainly up the mound of furniture to teeter on top. Goggs grabbed the loose end of the rein and hung on. All that remained was to collapse the pile of

furniture and Gloria would be left swinging by her neck from the beam.

"Scaffold away!" cried Goggs.

"No!" cried the boys.

"Away!" cried the drunken rabble of the Flying Horse, and turned the entire table on its side, bringing an avalanche of stools and kegs crashing down on their heads. The lynch-mob swore and rubbed their bruised heads.

Gloria fell. The leash went taut. The noose tightened round her neck. The inn-door opened and a chill evening wind sent the cigar butts rolling across the floor. Then the full weight of the dog was hanging on the leather rope; the rope was in Goggs' hands. He did not let go.

Not even when his boots were lifted clear off the floor.

Not even as the dog plummeted downward and Goggs rocketed towards the ceiling.

Only when he cracked his head on the beam did Magog Goggs, hangman, let go of the rein and fall, like a side of beef, to the floor. A cloud of sawdust rose up all around him. Trailing her leash rope and coughing, Gloria hurtled round and round the taproom barking and coughing and foaming a little at the mouth, as she grinned her foolish grin.

Clay cheered. Hal ran his hands through his hair. Goggs groaned and rolled over.

The Leader of the Night Watch, fetched there by the racket, stood in the open doorway and gazed around him. "What's amiss?" he said, in a voice of boomed authority. A sudden silence stuffed the room. Even the dog came to a standstill.

"Dog," mumbled Magog Goggs, though his mouth was pressed against the floor. "Mad dog," he said, sitting up, clutching his bloodied nose. "We were attempting to destroy a mad dog, officer."

"*She's not mad! She's not!*" wailed Clay.

"You again," said the Leader of the Watch. He turned to his patrolmen and told them to take the dog to the pound.

"Not true! Not true!" wailed Clay. "They were hanging her! They tried to hang her so they could drink her Dog tax!"

The Leader of the Watch looked around the room. Sober now, the drinkers were unwilling to meet his eye. They glanced down and shuffled their feet. "Let the animal be taken to the pound, until the truth be known."

"Save yourself the feed." In the darkest corner of the room, a man rose to his feet. He was part-shaven, with half a beard, half a moustache, half a head of hair. "I can oblige the City Fathers in this matter." He walked to the wooden pillar and tapped the largest of the notices pinned there. "I have the very skill you lack, gentlemen, and I am ready to rid you of this dangerous beast. What is more, I won't charge you one brown penny piece!"

9

A Picture of Ruin

*"You cannot! Arrest him! He's a
murderer!"*

Hal's mouth was so dry that the
words would hardly slip from his mouth,
but he coughed and said it again: "He's
a madman! We saw him do a murder!"

Never had the Flying Horse seen
such an evening of surprises. The

hubbub rose to a deafening roar.

"Silence!" boomed the Leader of the Watch, keeping a wary eye on the dog. He did not know what to think. It did not seem likely that so young a boy would make up such a lie, but neither did the accusation sound true. Soothingly he said: "Killing dogs is not murder, son, howsoever you like them."

"Not a dog! Not a dog, sir!" gasped Hal. "A farmer, name of Jellicoe. Up Ongar way! Send there! Ask about! On my troth, I swear it!"

All eyes turned on Skinner Hackett. His eyes flickered to right and left, behind half-closed lids. "There was an accident, yeah. The dog . . ." Hackett felt his way towards some story better than the truth. "The dog . . . that beast yonder . . . she went for Jellicoe. Yeah. That is what she did." He grew bolder as he found his lie. "These boys set the dog on to Jellicoe, bidding her 'rip out his throat'. I fired at the dog to kill it – to keep it off him. The bullet went wide and struck Jellicoe. As for dead, sir, he's no more dead than I am, sir. Dead? Huh!" He looked about him, supremely smug. "Tell you what, though. That dog is rabid. Seen it many a time in France, when I was with the army. That dog's a mad dog and must be put down this very night."

A large space cleared around the Golden Hound who sat, tongue lolling, mouth drooling at the smell of spilled ale. She stretched out on the floor, rolled over, cocked a leg and offered her stomach for Clay to scratch.

"She is not! She is not!" cried Hal, hating the tears that sprang to his eyes. "Ask anyone! Ask Mr Laguerre the artist!"

"And where would he be?" asked the Leader of the Watch, preparing to write down the name. (Privately he liked the look of the dog more than of Skinner, and he was willing to be persuaded.)

"In prison," said Clay. The Leader closed his notebook, and the skinner gave a loud, triumphant laugh.

"What about the lady in the forest, with the palace and the fairy pony who gave us a florin and sent us home in a coach?" cried Clay. Now the whole room was laughing. What preposterous lies would these boys tell next?

The Leader of the Watch sheathed his sword with a clash and a clack. "Who is the legal owner of the dog?"

"John Hay the offal man!" said Goggs, as quick as a wink. No one was going to demand two shillings from him for a dog with rabies.

"Ours! Ours!" cried Clay in despair. "We worked for her! We worked for months and weeks! We brought the two shillings to pay the Tax, but Father spent it . . ." His voice trailed away as his brother glared at him.

"So. The Tax has *not* been paid on this dog," the Watch Leader concluded. "That settles the matter. Let the dog be muzzled and shot . . ." Skinner swelled up with glee, like a ship whose sails fill with wind, ". . . but not in here. We want no more *accidents*."

The leather rein from which the noose had been made was wound around Gloria's nose to keep her from biting. A procession of watchmen, drinkers, boys, skinner and dog left the smoky fug of the Flying Horse and stepped outside into the sharp April night.

"What of my five shillings?!" Goggs wanted to know.

But by now Skinner was wearing his luck with a swagger. "You said yourself, the dog's not yours," he jeered. "And must I pay you five good shillings for the corpse of another man's dog? No, I'll pay nothing, thank you kindly. I am doing a service by ridding the City of a rabid dog. Ain't I?"

Despite the demolition work, lamps were burning brightly on the Bridge; the procession cast long, writhing shadows as they shambled across the river. In his misery, Hal looked down at the oily black of the Thames and began to think to himself, *We should never have fetched you off the ice, Gloria. I'd rather the river had taken you than these . . . these brutes. Then Jellicoe would not have robbed us. Hackett would not have laid hold on you. The shop would not have been wrecked. Laguerre might not be in prison . . .* They were just then passing the half-demolished house of the painter.

"The picture!" Hal said, stopping so abruptly that his brother bumped into him. "*The Rescue!*" He broke away from the rest and rushed over to the ruins of Laguerre's apartment. Its roof was off. Its upper storey had been dragged down. The front wall still stood to the height of a man's head, its front door concealing the tiled room where they had sat as Laguerre's models.

Hal threw himself against the door. It was locked. (How absurd to lock a house whose upper storey is gone.) He scrambled up, using the door latch for a step – up and over, into the living room *You would have plenty of light to paint by now,* copain, thought Hal, looking up through the no-ceiling at the night sky. Poor Laguerre! Hal had been so bound up with saving the dog that he had forgotten Laguerre, shut up in debtors' prison. Well, Gloria might be lost, but he and Clay could still rescue their friend!

The brick-strewn room looked so different that, at first, Hal could not remember quite where they had hidden the painting. Then he remembered the crack that yawned between window frame and wall each time a boat passed by. And yes! Yes! The bow window was still in place – still bulged out over the river. His fingers could feel the smoothness of canvas down the crack, but could not pluck it out.

"Hoi! You boy! Come forth from there!" bellowed the Leader of the Watch, banging on the door. "These buildings are condemned!" Clay did not

wait to knock but came scrabbling over the wall. "What are you doing, Hal? We have to save Gloria!"

"We have to save the painting!" Hal retorted. "It's Laguerre's only way to pay his debts. Remember what Lady Holland said?"

"How will that help Gloria?"

Hal gave a gasp of irritation. "It will not. But it will help Pierre."

For a moment the brothers looked at one another. Clay's little mouth was pursed with sorrow and resentment. Then he shook his head, crossed the room, climbed up on the window seat and began jumping up and down.

The wooden bench under his feet groaned. The glass panes rattled. Putty fell from the window frames. A mouse skittered out across the rubble-strewn floor. The Watch Leader clattered the door-latch. The stars glittered above them, and the black river gleamed, eel-like, below. The crack holding the hidden painting opened and shut like a fish's gill.

Perhaps the rain had already washed it blank. Perhaps the mice had already chewed it into holes. When Hal finally prised it free, his heart hardly rose at all. Lady Holland was not likely to want such a dusty web-covered scroll of crazed glaze. He unbolted the door and opened it to the Watch Leader. "There was this painting . . ." he began, explaining himself. "We promised Mr Laguerre to keep it safe. The lady in Epping said . . ."

A brick-barge moored under the Bridge swung out on the current and banged against the pillars with a dull boom. The noise drowned out his voice. Behind him, Clay, still standing on the window seat, leaned back against the window. The room shook –

as it had always shaken when boats grazed the Bridge. Only now, there was no upper storey pinning the building together.

The big bow window sagged; the glazing bars snapped like trellis wood. Sixteen panes of thick, bottle-end glass fell like fish scales into the river below.

And with them fell Clay.

10

Dogpaddle

"Son!" cried Goggs.

"Clay!" cried Hal.

"One in the water!" cried the
Leader of the Night Watch: he and his
men were often called on to pull poor
unfortunates from the Thames, drowned
or half-drowned.

The crowd on the Bridge was slow

to realise what had happened. Then, with a great scraping of boots, men scattered to either end of the Bridge and started down its steps. One called for a boat; one called for a rope. One said it was a mortal shame the shop that sold life-preservers had just been pulled down.

Hal ran over to the parapet, straining to see whether the current would wash his brother downriver. All the lamps were burning along the Bridge parapet, but their brightness only served to make the water below darker. Question was: would Clay be *above* the water or *under* it? Would he have cracked his head on the stone footings of the Bridge or was he even now trapped underwater among the wilderness of rubbish that caked the riverbed behind London Bridge?

The glistening river, unmoved, shouldered through the arches, no more disturbed by the fall of the boy than by the emptying of a chamber pot into her stream. Gloria, as slow as ever to grasp what was going on, felt the skinner measuring her back with the spread of his hand: measuring the length of her pelt. Mistaking this for stroking, Gloria lay down at the skinner's feet and offered her stomach to be rubbed. Skinner Hackett looked right and left then took out his knife, saying, "No time like the present."

Somewhere, above the noise of shouting, Gloria could hear the high, reedy voice of Clay: "Help! Somebody help me!" She wondered where it was coming from. Unwillingly, she rolled back on to her belly – and, in doing so, cut herself on the blade of Hackett's skinning knife. She gave a yelp. He made a wild slash at her throat, but she was too quick for him. Gloria had dodged many a blow in her time, and the pain made her think she was back with the Offal Man. Delivering a sharp bite to Hackett's knee, she leapt over the nearest wall to get away; the look in her eyes said, "Can't catch me!"

Then Gloria found herself falling, down and down, into the River Thames.

The water hit her, hard as ice, then treacherously opened up and swallowed her, down into a world of breathless blackness and bubbles.

"The dog has gone in after the boy!" yelled a watchman, and the running boots halted, while groans and cries of wonder echoed across the night river.

Hal bawled through cupped hands, *"Yes, Gloria! Good Gloria! Save Clay!"*

Clay, floundering between life and death, between stars and mud, between terror and unconsciousness, saw his dog hurtle down off the Bridge. He thought he was seeing the past. Well, people are supposed to see their whole past rush by them in the moment before dying: perhaps Clay was seeing his dog's past instead: the day the Offal Man threw her off the Bridge.

But then a huge wet haystack of golden fur bore down on him like Noah's Ark riding the Flood, and Clay was all tangled up with her, unable to tell his legs from hers. Both of them gasped for breath.

Gloria was hugely comforted to find Clay in the water as well. She tried to stand on his chest to lick him, as she would have done on shore, but Clay only sank. So she settled to swimming, head up, feet thrashing. Clay surfaced far behind her, gasping and choking.

"Help!" coughed Clay and then – in a moment of blinding inspiration – *"Fetch, Gloria! Fetch ME!"*

*   *   *

By the time the crowd on the bank had picked their way over the mudflat to the heap of fur and clothes, Gloria was the heroine of the day: the finest dog ever to have munched on a bone; a legend in fur mittens.

Skinner Hackett tried to argue that the deal had been struck, that the dog was his to skin and joint. But the customers of the Flying Horse Inn only picked him up and threw him off the Bridge steps into the muddy shallows. They did not want to be reminded of their shameful behaviour back at the inn. They did not want to be reminded of their one-time pets living wild now on the rubbish heaps or being worn as winter coats around the streets of Stepney.

Magog Goggs did not want to be reminded that he had spent the Dog Tax on buying a round of drinks. But he had. Luckily, Pierre Laguerre's portrait

pleased the sentimental Lady Holland
and she paid him twelve golden guineas
for it. Free of debt, Pierre immediately
paid the boys their two-shilling sitting
fee and a guinea each for saving his
bacon. Then, finding his rooms had been
demolished in his absence, he did not
look for new lodgings but left at once for
France. He would seek out (he said) the
clean light of the South, where nine
guineas buys a lot of oil paints, bread
and wine. He thought he might even get
himself a dog, since there was no foolish
Dog Tax in France.

Epilogue

Gloria in Excelsis

The dog days of summer are those last days of heat, when the roses wilt in the hedgerows, leaves curl like thirsty tongues, and the river flows through London full of harvest straw and field mice. The lakes shrink, rubbish heaps burst spontaneously into flame and the parks lie bleached pale and dreamy under a September sun.

Hal and Clay spent the dog days of
summer with Gloria, chasing sleepy
wasps on London Fields, fishing beneath
the arches, terrorising the stray cats,
watching the new houses go up on
London Bridge and the river lick its
cracked lips.

It was too hot for Gloria to wear her
livery – the jacket stitched with the
slogan:

This be ye dog
of Magog Goggs,
Hero of ye River.
Goggs' Emporium may be found
on London Bridge
at ye Sign of ye Golden Hound

Even so, people hailed them wherever
they went – the Goggs boys and their
heroic hound. Hal and Clay were in

Heaven, and Gloria (as the song goes) was in Excelsis.

She was the size and colour of a haystack, with a brain the size of a needle. But dim-witted as she was, Gloria knew better than to argue when people called her the finest and bravest dog in all London.

Author Note

London Bridge – the first to span the
Thames in London – was crammed with
buildings from end to end; it hardly
looked like a bridge at all. Its pilings
compressed the river into such a raging
torrent that passengers on boats would
get off rather than risk the rapids
beneath the Bridge. The strains on the

structure rocked and distorted the houses on it. Winters were much colder than now. Several times the Thames froze over: once, a fair was staged on the ice, complete with an ox-roast, and stage-coaches drove to and fro. The famous artist Hogarth carved a picture of his pet dog in the ice.

Not everyone was as lucky as Hogarth . . . After the Dog Tax of 1753 was introduced, not everyone could afford the luxury of a dog – two shillings was a lot of money then. Some owners were obliged to turn their pets out: hungry strays ganged together into packs.

But animal-skinners got rich, buying the pelts of unwanted dogs. Grisly advertisements like this one appeared throughout England:

This is to give notice that those persons who will hang their dogs and bring their skins to the King's Head shall receive for every skin not less than two shillings and six pence, and every mastiff or large mongrel five shillings. Ready money.
20th April 1753

Only very recently were dog licences abolished. After nearly 250 years, it became free once again to own a pet dog.